# Different Places, Different Words

Michelle Kelley

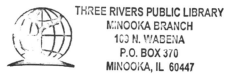

Rourke
Publishing LLC
Vero Beach, Florida 32964

www.rourkepublishing.com

PHOTO CREDITS: © Michael Howard: cover; © Brandon Laufenberg: page 4; © Jose Gil: page 5 (map); © Jason Stitt: page 5 (girls); © Joseph Justice: page 7; © Armentrout: page 9; © Lance Bellers: page 10; © Armentrout: page 11, 13, 15, 18, 21, 22; © sx70: page 12; © Lori Burwell: page 17; © Jeffrey Zavitski: page 19; © Ronen: page 20

Editor: Robert Stengard-Olliges

Cover design by Nicola Stratford

**Library of Congress Cataloging-in-Publication Data**

Kelley, Michelle.
  Different places, different words / Michelle Kelley.
    p. cm. -- (The world around me)
  ISBN 1-59515-993-2 (Hardcover)
  ISBN 1-59515-964-9 (Paperback)
1. Language arts (Elementary)--Juvenile literature. 2. Vocabulary--Juvenile literature.  I. Title.
  LB1576.K395 2007
  372.6--dc22
                              2006022159

**3 1561 00193 9879**

Printed in the USA

CG/CG

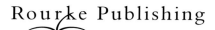

Rourke Publishing

www.rourkepublishing.com – sales@rourkepublishing.com
Post Office Box 3328, Vero Beach, FL 32964

# Table of Contents

# Soda or Pop?

Do you say soda or pop or soda pop? They all mean a fizzy, or **carbonated**, drink like root beer or cola.

We use different words for the same thing. The words are called **synonyms**.

You might use a certain word because that is the way your parents say it. You might say it because it is the way people in the **region** where you live say it.

# Hot Dogs or Franks?

When you go to a ball game or the park, do you ask for a frankfurter, or a hot dog. In Chicago people ask for a red hot. It will be a served on a roll and it may have mustard or relish on it. The name doesn't change the taste!

Do you ask for jimmies on your vanilla ice cream? Or do you ask for chocolate sprinkles?  Both add something special to your ice cream.

## Chips or Fries?

If you eat in a restaurant and order a **sandwich**, the menu may say it is served with chips. In many places chips is a different word for French fries.

If you are expecting to get a few potato chips on your plate you might be surprised with  a whole plate of French fries.

# Time and Place

Foods aren't the only words that people call by different names. We have synonyms for other things too. Do you say dollar or buck?

Do you call the place where your family buys food a grocery store or supermarket? Do you go to an ice cream shop or an ice cream parlor?

Some families gather to eat supper together. Some gather to eat dinner. Whatever you call it, it is a great time to eat together and share what you did that day.

# Creek or Brook?

In some regions of the country, people call a small river of water a brook. In other regions, people call it a creek.

No matter what you call it, it may be a great place to go fishing.

# Shore or Beach?

If you live near the ocean you might say you are going to the shore. Someone else might say they are going to the beach. No matter what you say, you can both see the ocean and play in the waves.

Do you call this animal a groundhog or a woodchuck? On Groundhog Day each February, people watch to see if this kind of animal comes out of **hibernation**. If it doesn't, they say the cold winter weather will continue.

Do you sit on a sofa or a couch?

Do you wear a cap or a hat?

Do you use a Kleenex or a tissue? We all use two or three words for the same thing. We all say synonyms!

# Glossary

**carbonated** (KAR buh nay ted) – with bubbles of carbon dioxide

**hibernation** (HYE bur nay shuhn) – a period of sleep some animals take during the winter

**region** (REE juhn ) – an area

**sandwich** (SAND wich) – two or more slices of bread with a filling between them

**synonyms** (SIN uh nim) – a word that means the same as another word

## Index

## Further Reading

Delpit, Lisa (ed.). *The Skin That We Speak*. New Press, 2002.
MacNeil, Robert. *Do You Speak American?* Doubleday, 2005.
Umsatter, Jack. *Where Words Come From*. Franklin Watts, 2002.

## Websites To Visit

www.pbs.org/speak

## About The Author

Michelle is a teacher who lives in Oviedo, Florida. She spends most of her free time with her husband Shaun and children Heather, 7, and Tyler, 11. She likes sports, cooking, and of course reading!